LOOKIN' FOR BIRD IN THE BIG CITY

Robert Burleigh

illustrated by Marek Los

Silver Whistle

Harcourt, Inc.

San Diego   New York   London

Requests for permission to make copies of any part of the work
should be mailed to the following address: Permissions Department,
Harcourt, Inc., 6277 Sea Harbor Drive, Orlando, Florida 32887-6777.

www.harcourt.com

Back cover photograph ©William P. Gottlieb from the Library of Congress Collection

Silver Whistle is a trademark of Harcourt, Inc., registered in
the United States of America and/or other jurisdictions.

Library of Congress Cataloging-in-Publication Data
Burleigh, Robert.
Lookin' for Bird in the big city/Robert Burleigh; illustrated by Marek Los.—1st ed.
p. cm.
"Silver Whistle."
Summary: A fictionalized account of the time when, as a teenage music student,
trumpeter Miles Davis spent many hours trying to find Charlie Parker in
New York City.
1. Davis, Miles—Juvenile fiction. [1. Davis, Miles—Fiction. 2. Trumpet players—
Fiction. 3. Jazz—Fiction. 4. Musicians—Fiction. 5. Afro-Americans—Fiction.]
I. Los, Marek, ill. II. Title.
PZ7.B9244Lo 2001
[E]—dc21   98-24270
ISBN 0-15-202031-4

H G F E D C B

Printed in Singapore

The illustrations in this book were done in pencil,
oil paint, and watercolor and were scanned and
finished in Photoshop and Painter on Macintosh 7100.
The display type was hand lettered.
The text type was set in Victoria Casual.
Printed and bound by Tien Wah Press, Singapore
This book was printed on totally chlorine-free
Nymolla Matte Art paper.
Production supervision by Sandra Grebenar
and Ginger Boyer
Designed by Lisa Peters

Miles Davis was a great American jazz muscian. When Miles was a teenager, he went to New York City to find and learn from the jazz master Charlie Parker, whom everyone called Bird. This is the story of what might have happened when young Miles first arrived in the "land of bebop."

For Brother Tom K.,
of the Monastic Order of Jazz (Cell 352)
—R. B.

For Agnieszka and Marcel
—M. L.

I was lookin' for Bird,
lookin' for Bird,
lookin' for Bird,

and heard
he might be jamming at a place
called Triple Doors.
But no.

Dip-dip, da-dee, bop-bop-daweeba, dooby-do.

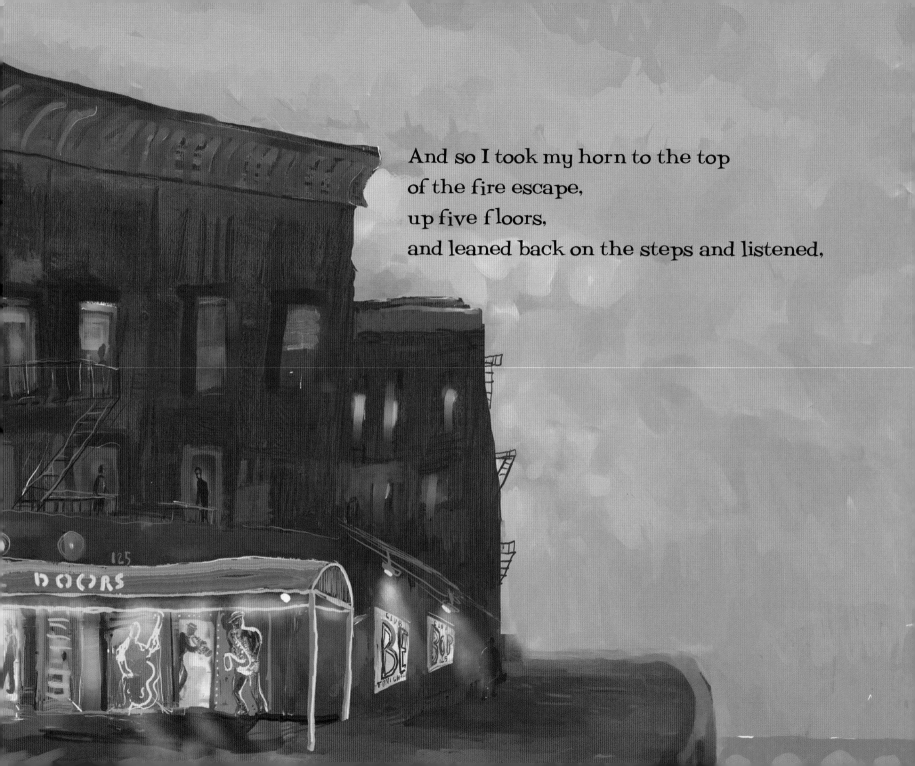

And so I took my horn to the top
of the fire escape,
up five floors,
and leaned back on the steps and listened,

to notes as staccato as stars,
and softer than the night.
Bird's horn was just like that,
and I wanted my music to fly like his
when I found him.

Sky-ee, dee-ah, dee-ah, do-dee, da-do.

Bird I wanted to find.
Never mind
I had the wrong address.

Instead, I took my horn
and walked out to the river,
and stood beside the railing of the bridge.

Notes came to me,
as jagged as the city skyline,
and far away as where the sun goes down,
'cause I wanted my music to soar as high as his,
and I had to be ready.

"Anyone around here know where Bird is?"
I asked,
but all they said was, "Who?"

And so I carried my horn
down into the subway, where
the train went rumbling through.

and I could feel notes
as cool as cave walls,
as hard as steel on steel,
'cause I knew Bird was somewhere,
waiting for me.

*Ca-chee, ca-chee,
bop, bop,
ca-chee,
ca-do.*

"You seen Bird?"
I asked the newsstand guy.
"Not I," he said.

And so I took the ferry
across the water,
and sat alone on deck,
and felt the wind
against my face and heard—

notes that clanged like buoy bells,
and tumbled like the whiteness of the wake,
'cause Bird's horn had those sounds inside it,
and I wanted them, too.

Zippa-wee-da,
wee-da,
dip;
da-wee,
da-wee.

"Bird been here?"
I asked the doorman at the New Café.
"Not today," he told me,
and so I waited under the awning,
in the rain,
and felt my horn in my hand,
and dreamed I was playing
notes for all the faces that went past,
hurrying, heads bent,
this way and that way,
'cause just like Bird,
from first to last,
I wanted the whole world in my music.

MADISON
SQUARE
GARDEN
PRESENTS

TICKETS CALL 2222

TONIGHT
Lady Day
Lester Young
Ray Brown,
Hank Jones
"BE-BOP"

VILLAGE VA

BE-BOP   B-DOO   B-DOO

NYU
JAZZ
CLUB

Washington
Square Park

presents
CHARLIE
"BE-BOP"
PARKER

• No Cover • No Min
NO RESERVATIONS

Dop-dop, skitteree, tic-tic, do-do-be-do.

"Bird, Bird, Bird,
where you gone?"
Don't know, don't know.
And so,

I sat up in my room
and watched the darkness coming on,

with notes as blue
as shadows on the walls,
and jazzy as the blink
of yellow building lights,
'cause I knew he was out there,
listening, too.

Ubadee, scat-skit, bopereebop, bop, ba-do.

I was lookin' for Bird,
lookin' for Bird.
Where, where?

And then one night—just like that—
he was there—▪
and I walked inside,
chest tight,
slow to the stage.

CHARLIE PARKER

THREE DEUCES

3 DEUCES

ROUSEL

3 DEUCES
presents
CHARLIE
"BE-BOP"
PARKER

No Cover • No Min

Was I ready?
I stopped.
I gazed into his eyes and knew I was,
and saw him nod,

and so I dipped my head,
and let my horn be me,
full of everything I knew,
city-light and city-shade,
and played,
and played,
and played,
finger-free,

notes that swooped like swallows,
notes as shrill as jays
and black as ravens—

Zip-de-ba, dip-dip-dip, de-beoo-de-boo—

till Bird behind me whispered,
"Take yourself a solo, kid."

And so I turned
and lifted my trumpet again—

and did.

Bop-bop-bop, be-bop, b-doo, b-doo,

this riff's for us, Bird,
for me
and for you.

afterWord

This story is loosely based on a time in the life of trumpeter Miles Davis. Miles was born in 1926 in Alton, Illinois. When he was a teenage music student, Davis's idol was the great saxophonist Charlie "Bird" Parker. During his first weeks in New York City, young Miles spent many hours (when not practicing) trying to find Parker. When they finally played together, Bird recognized the newcomer as a special voice in jazz. With Parker and others, Davis explored the jazz style called bebop, or bop. Bebop featured unusual rhythms and sometimes harsh-sounding chords. It also allowed the musicians a great amount of freedom in their playing. Later, Miles Davis—despite a sometimes troubled life—went on to become one of the most creative musicians in the history of American music. Two of his many famous recordings are *Kind of Blue* and *Miles Ahead.* He died in 1991.